MARY HOFFMAN has written more than 70 books for children and in 1998 was made an Honorary Fellow of the Library Association for services to children's library issues. She is also the editor of a quarterly children's book review called *Armadillo*. Her book *Song of the Earth* (Orion) was shortlisted for the Kurt Maschler Award in 1995. In 1992 *Amazing Grace*, her first book for Frances Lincoln, was selected for Child Education's Best Books of 1991 and Children's Books of the Year 1992, commended for the Kate Greenaway Medal, and included on the National Curriculum Reading List in 1996 and 1997. Its sequel, *Grace & Family*, was among Junior Education's Best Books of 1995 and was shortlisted for the Sheffield Libraries Book Award 1996. It was followed by *An Angel Just Like Me*, *A Twist in the Tail*, *Three Wise Women*, *Women of Camelot* and Grace story-book, *Starring Grace*. She has collaborated with Jackie Morris on *Parables: Stories Jesus Told* and *Miracles: Wonders Jesus Worked*.

PAM MARTINS trained at Brighton College of Art. After a period working on aircraft engines in the W.R.N.S., she began her career painting and sculpting. Cat subjects are her first love, captured in watercolour or designed on Cornish slate in her slate-carving workshop, which she opens to the public. Her work has been exhibited in the Mall Gallery in London and throughout the West Country, and each year she holds an exhibition of cat paintings for the Cat Protection League. Pam is married with three daughters and a son and lives in Salcombe, in South Devon. *How To Be a Cat* is her first illustrated book for Frances Lincoln.

DOMINO

DOZY

SLY

MISTY

PANSY

DOMINO

DOZY

SLY

MISTY

PANSY

For my sister, Phyllis – M.H.

For my family and my two cats Minnie and Hugo,
so often my working models – P.M.

How to be a Cat copyright © Frances Lincoln Limited 2001
Text copyright © Mary Hoffman 2001
Illustrations copyright © Pam Martins 2001

First published in Great Britain in 2001 by
Frances Lincoln Limited, 4 Torriano Mews
Torriano Avenue, London NW5 2RZ

First paperback edition 2002

British Library Cataloguing in Publication Data
available on request

ISBN hardback 0-7112-1261-9
ISBN paperback 0-7112-1901-X

Set in Bembo

Printed in Singapore

1 3 5 7 9 8 6 4 2

Mary Hoffman
Illustrated by Pam Martins

How to be a Cat

FRANCES LINCOLN

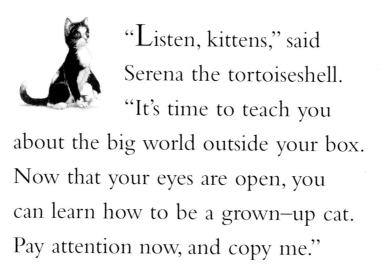

"Listen, kittens," said
Serena the tortoiseshell.
"It's time to teach you
about the big world outside your box.
Now that your eyes are open, you
can learn how to be a grown–up cat.
Pay attention now, and copy me."

"Lesson Number One is stretching and yawning. First, stretch your front legs as far as they will go. That's right. Now the back ones. Next, open your mouths as wide as you can, till I can see all your teeth. Good, Dozy - you're very good at yawning."

"Now," said Serena, "we're going to learn how to twine round people's legs. It's very useful when you want someone to hurry up and feed you. But you're not ready for human legs yet. We'll practise on this table."

"Washing is something you'll have to do a lot if you're going to be a proper cat. First, spit on your front paw like this. Then rub it round the back of your ear. Misty has the right idea.

Then twist your neck round and
try to reach every bit of your back
with your tongue. Finally, put one leg
up in the air and lick your ... oh dear,
Domino's fallen over."

"Now that you're all nice and clean, let's go and find some good places to climb. Pansy, you try the curtains. Sly, you hide behind the sofa and jump out on Misty and Dozy.

Domino, you try walking along the
back of the chair. Try not to look
undignified if you fall off."

"You're all looking sleepy again,"
said Serena, "and that's good. Curl up
in a heap and try having a catnap.
This laundry basket is a good place.
In fact, it looks so comfortable,
I think I'll join you."

"Mmmn. That was refreshing, wasn't it? Now it's time to practise stalking and pouncing. I'll stick my tail out and twitch it, then you can sneak up on me and pounce on it. You first, Pansy ..."

"You've all done very well. Now snuggle up
to me and I'll teach you the best lesson of all.
Grown-up cats are very good at
being relaxed and comfortable.
And when we are happy,
we make a rumbling noise
in our throats and it gets
louder and louder till it
sounds like an engine.
It's called purring.
That's right!
You're doing it!

What clever little cats!"

DOMINO

DOZY

SLY

MISTY

PANSY

DOMINO

DOZY

SLY

MISTY

PANSY

OTHER PICTURE BOOKS IN PAPERBACK
FROM FRANCES LINCOLN

AMAZING GRACE

Mary Hoffman
Illustrated by Caroline Binch

Grace loves to act out stories, so when there's the chance to play a part in Peter Pan,
Grace longs to play Peter. But her classmates say that Peter was a boy, and besides, he wasn't black...
With the support of her mother and grandmother, however,
Grace soon discovers that if you set your mind to it, you can do anything you want to.

Chosen as part of the recommended booklist for the National Curriculum Key
Stage 1, English Task 1997, Reading, Level 2
Suitable for National Curriculum English - Reading, Key Stage 1
Scottish Guidelines English Language - Reading, Level B

ISBN 0-7112-0699-6 £5.99

CAT IN THE DARK:
A FLURRY OF FELINE VERSE

Edited by Fiona Waters
Illustrated by Sophy Williams

Twelve mischievous poems celebrate every tail-twitch and whisker of the eternal cat –
from Aunt Agnes's overgrown Bengali Kitten to shabby old Tom, from the cautious Watercat
to Uncle Paul of Pimlico's feline choir. The poets include Margaret Mahy, Mervyn Peake
and Roger McGough, in a glorious night on the tiles for cat-lovers everywhere!

Suitable for National Curriculum English - Reading, Key Stages 1 and 2
Suitable for Nursery Education and for Scottish Guidelines English Language - Reading, Levels A and B

ISBN 0-7112-1476-X £5.99

Frances Lincoln titles are available from all good bookshops.
Prices are correct at time of publication, but may be subject to change.